Hector and th Cello

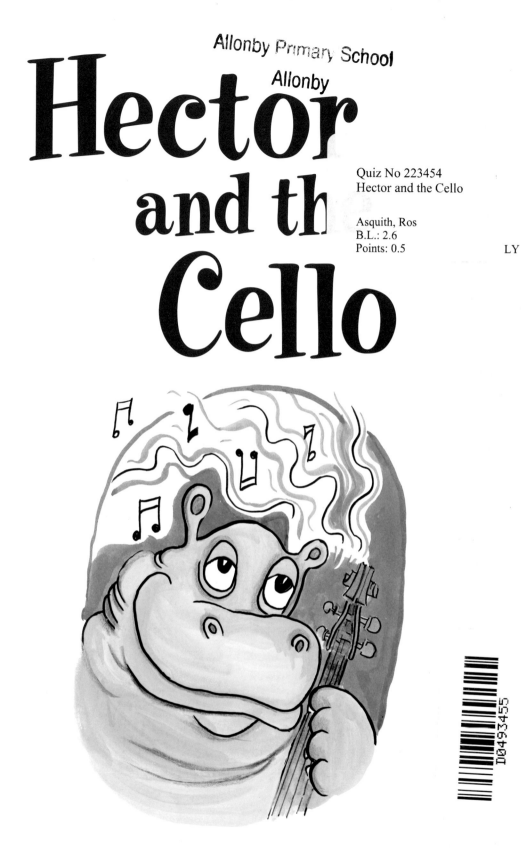

Written and illustrated by Ros Asquith

Collins

Hector the hippo wanted to play the cello more than anything else in the world.

But who in the wild, wet jungle would teach him?

Hector tramped through the jungle to find
a cello teacher. First he met a lion.
"I want to play the cello," said Hector.
"Whoever heard of a hippo playing the cello?"
roared the lion.
He roared so loudly that his mane fell off.

Hector picked up the lion's mane and draped it round
his neck.
It was going to be a chilly night in the wild, wet jungle.
On he tramped until …

… he met a leopard.

"I want to play the cello," said Hector.

"Whoever heard of a hippo playing the cello?" growled the leopard.

She growled so loudly that all her spots flew off.

Hector picked up the spots and stuck them on his back.
He might need a disguise in the wild, wet jungle.
On he tramped until …

… he met a rhino.

"I want to play the cello," said Hector.

"Whoever heard of a hippo playing the cello?"
snorted the rhino.

He snorted so loudly that his horn fell off.

Hector picked up the horn and went on his way.
He could blow on the horn if he got lost.
On he tramped until …

… he met a slithery snake.

"I want to play the cello," said Hector.

"SSSSSSSSSS. Hisssssssssss. SSSSTUPID! SSSSSILLY! SSSSAD!" hissed the snake.

She hissed so much that she slithered out of her skin.

Hector picked up the skin.

He might need a cloth to wipe his cello in the wild, wet jungle.

On and on he tramped until …

… he met a lyrebird.

"I want to play the cello," said Hector. "Please don't roar, or growl, or snort, or hiss."

"Do you have a cello?" asked the lyrebird.

"No," said Hector. "But I have a lion's mane, a leopard's spots, a rhino's horn and a snake's skin. Will that buy me a cello and some lessons?"

"Of course!" said the lyrebird, who was a good musician.

Every single day for two years, Hector tramped happily
through the wild, wet jungle for his cello lessons.

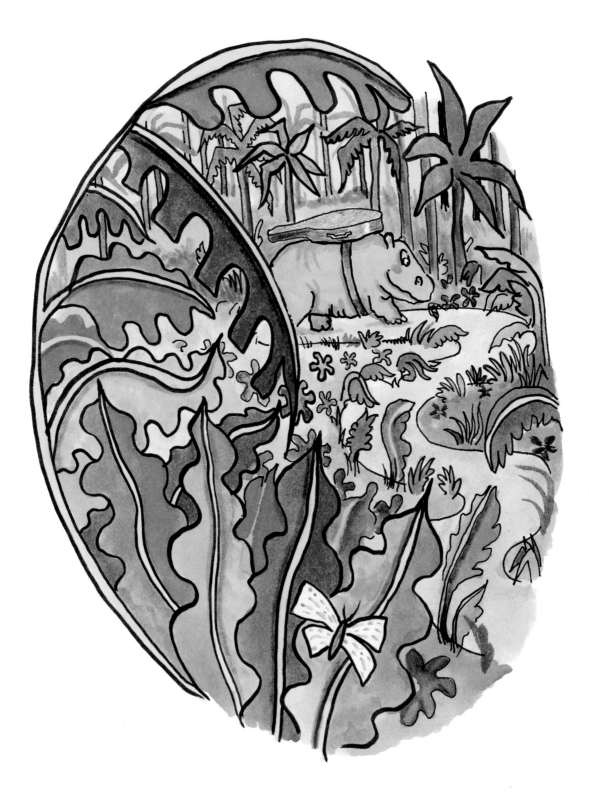

Two years and one day later, there was a grand concert.
All the animals from the jungle came.

Hector started to play.
The sound was so sweet ...

The lion roared for more.

The leopard growled with glee.

The rhino snorted with surprise.

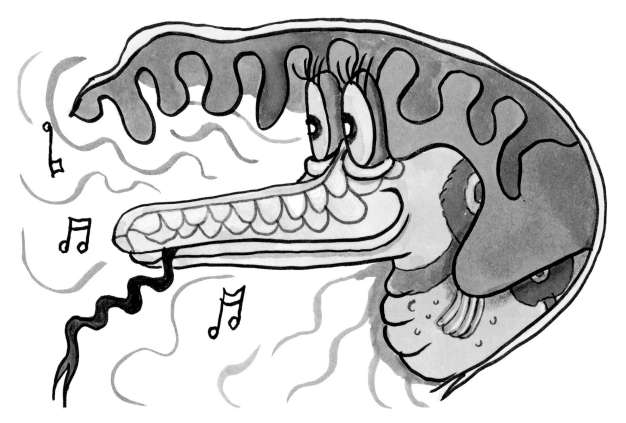

The snake hissed with happiness.

So the musician gave the lion
his mane back.

He gave the leopard
her spots back.

He gave the rhino
his horn ...

... and the snake
her skin.

In the wild, wet jungle the animals
made music until midnight.

Hector and the Cello

1

2

5

6

3

4

7

8

✿ Ideas for guided reading ✿

Learning objectives: Retell stories, giving the main points in sequence, and notice the difference between written and spoken forms; become aware of character and dialogue, e.g. by roleplaying parts; learn and recite simple texts, with actions, and reread from the text; act out well known stories; explore animal and musical instrument sounds using instruments and voice.

Curriculum links: Music: Exploring sounds; classroom instruments; combining sounds to make music; Science: Animals; ICT: Using text and tables to develop ideas

Interest words: hippo, cello, lion, mane, leopard, spots, rhino, horn, snake, skin

Word count: 439

Getting started

This book can be read over two sessions

- Look at the front cover. What kind of animal is Hector? What is a cello?
- Walk through the book to p21, turning pages in order and identify other animals.
- Write the names of the animals (*hippo, lion, leopard, rhino, snake, lyrebird*) on a whiteboard; check initial and final sounds (the final sound of snake is k).
- Discuss what the story might be about. Read pp2-5 together.

Reading and responding

- Read through the book together as a group. Leave pp22-23 till later. As children read, praise and prompt good use of decoding strategies.
- Return to the beginning and encourage children to reread independently, using knowledge of the story to work out unfamiliar words and using one to one matching.
- Listen to each child read independently and observe their ability to tackle unfamiliar words.